ZAPATO POWER
FREDDIE RAMOS ADDS IT ALL UP

JACQUELINE JULES   art by MIGUEL BENÍTEZ

Albert Whitman & Company
Chicago, Illinois

Don't miss the first seven **Zapato Power** books!

Freddie Ramos Takes Off
Freddie Ramos Springs into Action
Freddie Ramos Zooms to the Rescue
Freddie Ramos Makes a Splash
Freddie Ramos Stomps the Snow
Freddie Ramos Rules New York
Freddie Ramos Hears It All

Library of Congress Cataloging-in-Publication
data is on file with the publisher.

Text copyright © 2019 by Jacqueline Jules
Illustrations copyright © 2019 by Albert Whitman & Company
Illustrations by Miguel Benítez
First published in the United States of America
in 2019 by Albert Whitman & Company
ISBN 978-0-8075-9539-8 (hardcover)
ISBN 978-0-8075-9556-5 (ebook)
Printed in the United States of America
10 9 8 7 6 5 4 3 2 1 LB 24 23 22 21 20 19

For more information about Albert Whitman & Company,
visit our website at www.albertwhitman.com.

100 Years of Albert Whitman & Company
Celebrate with us in 2019!

To everyone who has ever felt
a little bit "different"—JJ

Contents

1. Messed Up Morning 1

2. Pink Lunch Bag 10

3. Too Much Rain 19

4. Grown-Ups! 29

5. Playground Ghost 39

6. Amy Is Fast! 50

7. Where Is Amy? 61

8. Sliding to the Rescue 73

1. Messed Up Morning

Mom made oatmeal with raisins.

"A treat, Freddie!" she said. "*Un desayuno caliente.*"

Mom was so proud of herself for making a hot breakfast, I didn't have the heart to say I liked crunchy cereal with milk better. Oatmeal is too mushy to wake me up in the morning.

"Mmmm," Mom said as she lifted her spoon. "I should do this more often."

Mom had cooked because she wanted me to pass my math test. She was sure that a hot breakfast would help me count without my fingers. Mom must have gotten that idea from my teacher, Mrs. Blaine. Last week, they had a meeting about my math grades. Ever since, Mom's been changing things like breakfast and bedtime because good food and sleep are supposed to make kids think better at school.

"WHEET! WHEET!" My guinea pig, Claude the Second, started squealing. Hearing us talk about oatmeal must have made him hungry.

"Do we have carrots?" I asked Mom. "Claude the Second needs a treat too."

"*Sí*. But hurry. You don't want to be late. *Hoy no*."

Getting dressed wasn't as easy as feeding my guinea pig. I couldn't remember what

I wore for my last math test. Whatever it was, I didn't want to wear it again. I pulled a green shirt from the very back of my drawer. Was green lucky like a four-leaf clover? It was worth a try. I decided to wear green socks too.

Then I went to the front door to pick up my sneakers. That's the best part of every morning. My purple zapatos are special. With my superpowered purple sneakers, I can run ninety miles an hour. I can jump really high. I can hear things from far away. They give me everything I need to be a superhero. And when they weren't on the mat by the door, my heart stopped.

Where were my purple zapatos? They weren't by the sofa or under the kitchen table either. I rushed back to my room to search. I couldn't go to school until I found them.

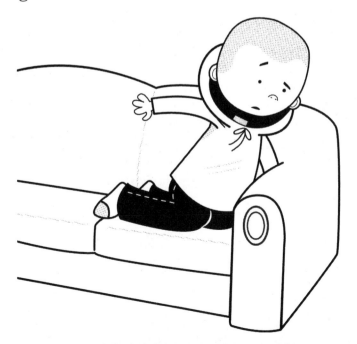

Even Mom would agree. It was too cold outside to wear flip-flops, and I didn't have anything else for my feet.

"Freddie?" Mom asked from my doorway. "Where are you?"

"Under the bed," I called back. "Looking for my sneakers."

"I cleaned them!" Mom said. "*¡Mira!* No more mud!"

I didn't know muddy shoes were bad for your brain. Maybe that was something else Mrs. Blaine had told Mom.

"*Gracias.*" I put my shoes on and raced out the door before Mom could find any other ways to help me.

Outside, I put on my silver

goggles and touched my wristband. That turned on my super speed for zooming down the steps to Starwood Elementary.

ZOOM! ZOOM! ZAPATO!

At the school playground, I did some extra laps to calm down for my test.

 **ZOOM! ZOOM! ZAPATO!**

The third time around, I saw some kids teasing a girl by the swings. She was wearing pink sunglasses.

One of the boys shouted at her.

"Let us see your eyes!"

"NO!" she shouted back. "My eyes are none of your business!"

The bullies looked short, like first graders. But there were five of them and one of me. I didn't like those numbers. Luckily, I had three superpowers. One Freddie and three superpowers equaled four on the fingers of my left hand. That made it five to four. Those numbers were better.

BOING! BOING! BOING!

I touched my wristband to turn on my super bounce and landed right in the middle of the bullies.

2. Pink Lunch Bag

My Zapato Power covered me in a cloud of invisible smoke. The mean kids didn't see me until I was standing right in front of them. They were so shocked, they scattered like ants. *¡Fue genial!*

The girl with the sunglasses ran away too. That didn't make me feel as great. She was in such a hurry,

she dropped her pink lunch bag.
Now I had to find her to give it
back. Superheroes have to finish
their jobs.

ZOOM! ZOOM! ZAPATO!

When I got inside, I saw all the
first graders sitting down, lined
up against the wall, waiting for
the bell to ring. It should have
been easy to find one girl wearing
pink sunglasses. Except it wasn't.
Sunglasses are for outdoors, not
indoors.

Everything had happened so fast, I never got a good look at the girl on the playground. Now I was stuck in the first-grade hall, holding a pink lunch bag with glittery princesses all over it.

"Hey, Freddie!" Gio, my next-door neighbor, waved at me. He was a first grader. Maybe he could help.

I showed Gio the lunch bag.

"It belongs to Amy," Gio told me.

Sometimes asking questions is better than running around.

"Are you sure?" I asked.

He pointed. "Look at the name."

Gio was right. It said "Amy" in big blue letters, right above the princesses. Now we were getting somewhere.

"Do you know Amy?"

"She's new." Gio shrugged. "And she doesn't talk to me."

"Just you?" I asked. That didn't seem right. Most people liked Gio.

"She doesn't talk to anybody." Gio looked over the line of first graders. "See the girl at the very end?"

I sure did. She was hugging her

knees and had her head down.

"Is that Amy?"

Gio nodded. I walked down the hall with the pink lunch bag, just as the first bell rang. Everybody got up, including Amy. But she kept her eyes on the floor.

"I found your lunch," I said to the top of her head.

"Thanks," she mumbled, taking the bag without ever looking up.

She hurried into Room 12 with Gio and a bunch of other first graders while I stood there wondering. Why wouldn't Amy look at me?

The second bell rang. Ugh! Now I was going to be late to class.

ZOOM! ZOOM! ZAPATO!

Using my superpowers meant being in the hallway a lot. I was always fast, and my Zapato Power smoke covered me until I slowed down. But today the principal, Mrs. Connor, just happened to be there when I stopped running. *¡Qué mala suerte!*

"Freddie?" Mrs. Connor asked. "Why aren't you in your classroom?"

"I'm sorry." I looked up at Mrs. Connor with my saddest eyes.

"That's what you said yesterday, Freddie." Mrs. Connor sighed.

She took me by the arm to Mrs. Blaine's desk.

"I found Freddie in the hallway," Mrs. Connor said. "Keep an eye on him."

My teacher thanked Mrs. Connor and handed me the math test. Everyone else in my class had their pencils on their paper, already working. This wasn't good. I needed more time, not less.

Mrs. Blaine put a hand on my

shoulder. "Take a deep breath, Freddie. Just sit down and do your best."

How could I do that? A math test was not like counting bullies on the playground. My paper had 386 + 207. I couldn't count that on my fingers if I had all day!

"Time's up!" Mrs. Blaine walked down the aisles, collecting the tests. I had only one thing right on my paper for sure. It was my name.

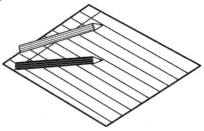

3. Too Much Rain

I went to lunch in a grumpy mood. My friends noticed.

"*¿Qué pasa?*" Maria asked. "You never frown, Freddie."

"Are you sad because of indoor recess?" Jason looked out the window at the pouring rain.

I didn't tell my friends about my math grade. It was another secret

in my life, like my super zapatos.
Secrets aren't easy. Sometimes
Maria seemed suspicious when I
disappeared in a puff of smoke.

Geraldo had noticed the
flashing buttons on the
purple wristband I wear to
control my superpowers. And
once, Jason saw me in my silver
goggles. He told me I looked
like a crime fighter—just
what I want to be.

"Cheer up, Freddie."
Jason said. "We'll have fun
anyway."

After we ate, we went back to

the classroom to play with the stuff in Mrs. Blaine's blue crates. Geraldo and Jason were excited because Mrs. Blaine had a new game. It was a money game. I'd never played it before. That's why I didn't say no when Maria asked me to be the banker. Big mistake.

"Freddie!" Geraldo complained. "You gave me the wrong change."

Being the banker meant subtracting and adding in my head. I couldn't

do it fast, and I couldn't do it right. For the first time ever, I was glad to see recess end.

"Don't feel bad, Freddie," Jason said as we picked up the game. "You tried your best."

Everybody knows Jason as the kid who cried over broken pencils. All of a sudden, I wondered if that was fair. Jason hadn't cried in school since last year.

"Thanks," I told him. "You're a good friend."

The rain was still coming down at the end of the day. I didn't have an umbrella, so I tied the hood on my sweatshirt. I put on my silver goggles too.

ZOOM! ZOOM! ZaPaTO!

I headed for the stairs between Starwood Elementary and Starwood Park Apartments.

At the bottom, I saw a girl with a pink umbrella, carrying a pink lunch bag. Amy! Would she talk to me about the bullies? Maybe I could help.

ZOOM! ZOOM! ZAPATO!

OOPS!

Stopping short after going ninety miles an hour is a lot easier when the pavement is dry, not slippery from rain. Instead of just catching up with Amy, I slid into her.

"Sorry!" I said.

She wasn't hurt, only wet and angry.

"You did that on purpose!" Amy said.

I picked up her dripping umbrella. It didn't make Amy forgive me.

"Why won't people leave me alone?" She stamped her foot in a puddle.

I looked at her face under the umbrella. She was wearing sunglasses in the pouring rain. Why?

It was a question I should have kept to myself. As soon as I asked it, Amy had one for me.

"Why are you wearing goggles?" She pointed at my face.

The answer had two parts. My silver goggles protected my eyes when I ran at super speed. They also made me feel like a hero. I couldn't tell Amy either part. No one knew about my superpowered sneakers except Mr. Vaslov, my friend who'd invented them.

When I didn't answer, Amy turned her pink umbrella around and ran away.

"Wait!" I called through the rain.

But she was gone in a flash, and my head was getting soaked. Maybe Mr. Vaslov knew Amy and could tell me more about her. He

knew everybody at Starwood Park.
Besides being the best inventor in
the world, Mr. Vaslov was the man
who took care of the buildings.
On a rainy day like this, he was
probably in his toolshed.

ZOOM! ZOOM! zapato!

I knocked on Mr. Vaslov's door.
Before I could say anything, he had
a question.

"Freddie, what are you doing out
in the rain?"

4. Grown-Ups!

For some reason, grown-ups like kids to be dry, not wet. Mr. Vaslov spent way too much time wiping my head with a paper towel.

"You're dripping everywhere," he said.

Mr. Vaslov's paper towel was strong like the TV commercials say, but it wasn't too soft. I was glad

when he felt I was dry
enough for talking.

"Yes, I know Amy
Escobar. Her family
just moved here from
Chicago."

"She's not very friendly," I said.

"Why do you say that?" Mr. Vaslov
picked up a tiny screwdriver and
leaned over his worktable. He liked
to talk and work at the same time.

"She won't look at people," I said.

"Maybe she's shy," Mr. Vaslov
suggested.

Shy meant being scared. What was
Amy scared of? I asked Mr. Vaslov if

he knew.

"Does it matter?" Mr. Vaslov answered. "You can still be nice to her."

I watched Mr. Vaslov unscrew a metal box and take measurements with a tiny ruler. One day, I wanted to be an inventor, just like Mr. Vaslov. I dreamed of making a backpack with a jet engine or a time travel machine. At least until I saw him write numbers on a pad of paper.

"Do you need math to make inventions?" I asked.

"Math helps," Mr. Vaslov answered. "Scientists use it all the time."

"Then I'm in BIG trouble!"

Mr. Vaslov put down his screwdriver. "What's wrong, Freddie?"

"Too many things need math!" My voice was loud. Mr. Vaslov blinked.

"I can't play board games. I can't make a time machine! And now my report card is going to get even worse!"

"Why is that?" Mr. Vaslov asked quietly.

I tried to explain in a softer voice. "Right now, my report card has four main parts. I get B's or better in everything except math. But if science needs math, too, then soon I will have two bad grades—half of my report card!"

"Mmm," Mr. Vaslov said. "How do you know it's half?"

"Because half of four is two," I said.

"Are you sure?" Mr. Vaslov asked.

I counted on my fingers. Yes, I was sure.

Mr. Vaslov had another question for me. "Have you talked to anyone at school about this?"

"Way too much!" I complained. "Mrs. Blaine called in a special teacher to give me a long test. It was really hard."

Mr. Vaslov patted my shoulder. "Don't worry, Freddie. Other kids have trouble in math. They get extra practice, and things work out."

Extra practice? That didn't sound fun.

Mr. Vaslov checked his watch. "Better go home, Freddie. Your mom must be wondering where you are."

"No." I sighed. "Mom is wondering how I did on my math test."

"Be brave, Freddie." Mr. Vaslov opened the door to the toolshed for me.

It was still raining. Too bad. It was the one time I wanted to go slow, but if I did, I'd get drenched.

ZOOM! ZOOM! ZAPATO!

Just like I thought, Mom was at the door, waiting for me.

"Freddie! *¡Tengo buenas noticias!*" She clapped her hands. "Mrs. Blaine called!"

When a teacher calls, it's bad news, not good news. Mom was confused.

"She has a great idea for you," Mom explained. "Extra math practice!"

That's what Mr. Vaslov said. Now I had three grown-ups who wanted me to do the same thing. Why did they think it would help?

Mom continued. "Mrs. Blaine says that some students need more time to understand math. She has helped me set up after-school lessons for you with Mr. Newton in Room 12."

Room 12? That was Amy and Gio's classroom in the first-grade hall. What would Geraldo and Maria say? They complained when I made mistakes as banker in the money game. Would they tease me for having to go back to first-grade math?

5. Playground Ghost

The rain was over the next morning. My math problems weren't. Amy's problems weren't over either. The same kids were teasing her by the swings on the playground. This time, they had pulled off her sunglasses.

"Give them back!" she screamed.

A taller boy was waving the

sunglasses over Amy's head. She jumped to grab them. When that didn't work, she covered her eyes and ran off.

The boys laughed. Too mean! They shouldn't get away with that.

ZOOM! ZOOM! ZAPATO!

I swiped the glasses right out of the taller boy's hand. He didn't see anything except a puff of smoke.

"What's going on?" he asked. "Does the playground have a ghost?"

I grinned. If those mean kids thought Starwood Elementary had a ghost, I was happy to give them one.

ZOOM! ZOOM! ZAPATO!

I did circles around the bullies, going so fast, all they could see was a ring of smoke.

ZOOM! ZOOM! ZAPATO!

The first-grade bullies froze in place.

ZOOM! ZOOM! ZAPATO!

I ran off and slipped into my classroom just as the second bell rang. I felt good until I looked at my hand and saw I was still holding Amy's pink sunglasses. Could I sneak back out to return them? Not a chance.

"Freddie!" Mrs. Blaine called. "Please sit down. Class is about to begin."

As usual, we had math first thing. What a rotten way to start the day!

Mrs. Blaine pulled me away from my desk to sit at a computer in the back of the classroom.

"Try this math game," Mrs. Blaine

whispered, while the rest of my class started on a worksheet. "It will help you understand multiplication better."

A computer game was way more fun than getting a headache from a sheet of numbers. I got to wear headphones and hear a happy voice tell me "good job" every

few minutes. The only bad part was Geraldo's face staring at me when we went out for recess.

"Why is Mrs. Blaine being so nice to you?" he asked. "No one else gets to play with the computers during class. They're for free time."

Playing on a computer was great. Telling my friends why, was not.

"Mrs. Blaine called my mom. She says I'm not learning math the way other kids do. I need extra help."

"Have you been failing tests?" Maria asked. "How many?"

I raised four fingers. That was easier than saying it out loud.

Geraldo whistled. "Whew! I thought you were smart, Freddie."

"I did too," Maria said.

"Don't pick on him," Jason
defended me. "Freddie is smart
about other things."

For a minute, Geraldo and Maria
looked at Jason like he had just
stepped out of a spaceship. I bit
my lip, waiting to hear what would
come next.

Geraldo shrugged. "I wish I could play with computers during math."

"No reason to be mean," Jason said firmly.

"He's right," Maria agreed.

And that was the end of it. If only things were so easy for Amy.

I looked across the playground and saw Gio. If he was there, Amy might be nearby. I could return her sunglasses.

ZOOM! ZOOM! ZAPATO!

I arrived in a puff of smoke. Gio

 didn't see me right away. He was with two other kids, busy doing something I didn't like. He was staring at Amy. She was holding her right hand over her eyes.

"Just show us," Gio said. "We won't hurt you."

"Show you what?" I asked.

That was enough to break up the circle. Amy ran off like a squirrel. Gio turned to me.

"Why did you do that?" he asked.

"Why did you?" I asked back.

"Everyone says Amy's eyes are different. I wanted to see."

"You weren't being nice," I told Gio.

"*Lo siento.*" Gio hung his head.

Gio was not a mean kid. He was just curious. The bad thing was that I understood. I was curious too.

6. Amy Is Fast!

There were still a few minutes of recess left. Enough time for a quick zoom around the school to find Amy and return her sunglasses.

I checked the library and the nurse's office. No Amy.

ZOOM! ZOOM! ZAPATO!

I searched the classrooms and the gym. I even peeked into Mrs. Connor's office to see if Amy was there. She wasn't. Big relief. No one likes the principal's office, not even superheroes.

ZOOM! ZOOM! ZAPATO!

Where could Amy be? The only places I didn't check were the girls' bathrooms. If Amy was hiding in one, she was safe from the bullies and from me.

ZOOM! ZOOM! ZAPATO!

Recess was over, and kids were coming in through the doors from the playground. I headed back to my class. On the way, I passed Room 12. That's when I finally saw Amy! She dashed around the corner and into her classroom. *¡Muy rápido!*

That got me thinking. How fast was Amy? Every time I saw her, she disappeared before I could blink. Did Starwood Elementary have two kids with super speed?

What did Gio mean when he said Amy's eyes were different? Did they give her a special power? Was Amy shy, or was she hiding a superpower behind her sunglasses? I took them out of my pocket to look them over. Could they be a superhero mask like my silver goggles?

I worried the whole afternoon. First, about Amy. Then, about Mr. Newton. Would I like extra math lessons? Was Mr. Newton nice? Not all teachers are nice. Sometimes they make you do more work than your head can handle. Sometimes they frown and sigh.

By the time the final bell rang, I was not feeling like a boy with super speed. My feet dragged on the ground. Mrs. Connor spotted me in the hallway going to Room 12. She said I looked like I was carrying cement.

"Don't be afraid, Freddie. Mr. Newton is a good teacher. You'll like him."

How did the principal know what was going on? Did Mrs. Blaine talk to her too? How many people knew my brain had trouble figuring out math?

"A learning problem can slow you down a little," Mrs. Connor said. "But it doesn't have to stop you from doing well in life."

She put her hand on my shoulder and walked me all the way into Room 12, making sure I didn't escape. Mrs. Connor never takes chances with me.

Mr. Newton was in the back of the room with a bunch of brightly colored plastic blocks. They were different shapes and sizes.

"Sit down, Freddie," Mr. Newton said. "Let's learn how numbers work."

Math made a lot more sense with blocks than on a piece of paper.

Block counting was like finger counting, except I didn't have to worry about running out of things to touch.

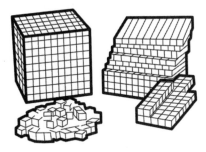

Mr. Newton explained that some people need to connect numbers to something real.

"Stick with me, Freddie," he said. "I know lots of tricks to make math easier."

We were having a good time until Mrs. Connor charged into the room.

"Mr. Newton!" Mrs. Connor was breathless. "Have you seen Amy Escobar?"

He looked at his watch. "Not since the final bell. Why?"

"Her mother just called. Amy did not come home from school."

Mrs. Connor shook her hands up and down like she was trying to dry them off.

"I'm sorry, Freddie. Your lesson must be cut short."

That was okay. Mr. Newton and I could play with blocks another time. Today, I had a chance to be a hero.

I left the building with Mr. Newton and Mrs. Connor. They thought I was heading up the steps to my own home in Starwood Park Apartments. They were wrong. I was on my way to find Amy.

ZOOM! ZOOM! ZAPATO!

7. Where Is Amy?

The first thing I did was take
a loop around Starwood Park
Apartments. Amy was supposed to
go up the steps and down the short
path to the buildings. If something
had made her change her mind,
maybe there was a clue on one of
the sidewalks.

BINGO! There was a clue! Except

I didn't like it much. Amy had dropped her pink lunch bag again. Now I had two things to return— her sunglasses and her lunch bag.

ZOOM! ZOOM! ZAPATO!

Things were not making sense. Why did Amy keep dropping her lunch bag? Why didn't she go home? And where was she? I rubbed the buttons on my purple wristband so I could use my super hearing. I needed all my powers working.

ZOOM! ZOOM! ZAPATO!

I kept running in circles until finally my super hearing helped me out. STOMP! It was the sound of a foot coming down on the sidewalk. On the other side of Building H, someone was shouting and stamping the ground.

"WHERE AM I?"

I recognized that voice. It was the same voice that had yelled at me in the rain, from under a pink umbrella. Amy!

ZOOM! ZOOM! ZAPATO!

But when I caught up with her, she started running away.

"Wait!" I called. "I have your lunch bag and your sunglasses."

That made Amy stop. "My sunglasses?" she said, without turning around. "Give them back!" She stretched out her hand.

I gave her the glasses.

"The grown-ups are looking for you," I said. "Your mom called the school."

"Well, I'm looking for them!" Amy pushed her sunglasses onto her face and stamped her foot again. "This place has too many buildings."

It was true. Starwood Park had ten buildings that all looked the same and lots of sidewalks. It would be easy to get lost if you were a first grader who didn't know your way around.

"Why didn't you go straight home?" I asked.

"The bullies," she answered. "I was trying to get away."

"And you went in the wrong direction," I finished.

Now I understood. Amy probably dropped her lunch bag to go faster.

She was a good runner, but she didn't have super speed.

"What building do you live in? Can I show you the way home?"

I may not know how to count without blocks or fingers, but I do

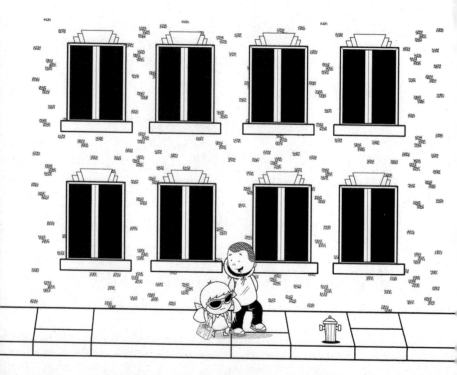

know how to get around Starwood Park. On the way to 15C, where Amy lived, we talked.

"You're a lot nicer than the other kids," she told me.

"Are they all mean?" I asked.

"No," she said. "Some kids just stare."

"At what?" I was still curious, just like Gio.

"My eyes," Amy said. "They don't match."

"Match?" I had never heard that. "What do you mean?"

"I have one blue eye and one brown eye."

So that's what Amy was hiding.

When we arrived at 15C, Amy's mother ran out. There was the usual crying and shouting that happens when kids come home late. I got out of there.

ZOOM⚡ZOOM⚡zapato⚡

I went straight to Mr. Vaslov's toolshed. He was always a good person to talk things over with.

"Are you sure you have this right, Freddie?" he asked. "Amy's eyes may not be the problem."

"Why not?" I asked.

know how to get around Starwood
Park. On the way to 15C, where
Amy lived, we talked.

"You're a lot nicer than the other
kids," she told me.

"Are they all mean?" I asked.

"No," she said. "Some kids just
stare."

"At what?" I was still curious, just
like Gio.

"My eyes," Amy said. "They
don't match."

"Match?" I had never heard of
that. "What do you mean?"

"I have one blue eye and one
brown eye."

"Amy sees perfectly well," Mr. Vaslov told me.

"I'm glad," I said.

"And she sees how other people look at her," Mr. Vaslov added.

"Because her eyes are different?"

Mr. Vaslov nodded his bushy gray head.

"That's not fair," I said.

"No," Mr. Vaslov agreed.

I remembered how I felt about needing extra math help. *Me sentí mal.*

"Everybody is different in some way," I said.

"True," Mr. Vaslov answered. "Amy needs to know she's not alone. She needs to know others care for her just the way she is."

That's what Jason did when he told Geraldo to stop teasing me. Could I do that for Amy? I wasn't sure.

8. Sliding to the Rescue

At school the next morning, Mrs. Connor called me into her office. We sat down at a round table, opposite each other.

"Don't look so scared, Freddie," she said. "You're not in trouble."

Then what was I doing there?

"I mean it, Freddie," Mrs. Connor said. "Please relax."

Why do grown-ups tell you to relax when they do things to make you nervous?

"I want to talk about Amy," Mrs. Connor began. "You found her yesterday."

I didn't let go of my breath. If Mrs. Connor wanted to know how I'd heard Amy from the other side of a building, this was going to be tricky.

"Are you friends?" Mrs. Connor asked.

"Sort of. She just moved here."

Mrs. Connor nodded. "Amy hasn't had time to make friends."

"And kids are being mean to her," I added.

"Those students have been disciplined." Mrs. Connor frowned. "We will be watching them."

"They shouldn't have made fun of Amy because she's different," I said.

"You're right," Mrs. Connor agreed. "So what can we do to help?"

All I could think of was what Mr. Vaslov had said.

"We need to show Amy she's not alone. That it's okay. Nobody needs to match."

As soon as I said that, Mrs. Connor jumped out of her chair and clapped her hands like she'd won a prize.

"GREAT IDEA, FREDDIE!"

She picked up a paper off her desk. "Take a look at this!"

It was a flyer for something called "Two Different Shoes Day." I liked the picture, which showed a smiling girl wearing one green sneaker and one blue sneaker.

"This has been on my to-do list for a while," Mrs. Connor explained. "What do you think?"

"Of what?"

Sometimes grown-ups get excited about stuff and forget to tell kids what they're talking about.

"Two Different Shoes Day," Mrs. Connor said. "A day to celebrate being different, being an individual, and not being the same as everyone else."

It wasn't a bad idea. Amy might feel more comfortable with her eyes if she saw everyone else at Starwood

Elementary not matching either. But I couldn't do it.

"Does it have to be shoes?" I asked Mrs. Connor.

She looked surprised. "Why?"

I stared at the floor. It wasn't just that I loved my superpowered purple sneakers. I didn't have two different pairs of shoes.

"Could it be socks?" I asked. "Everybody has more than one color of socks."

Mrs. Connor's eyes flashed for a moment. She smiled.

"Of course!" Mrs. Connor said. "Socks would make it easier

for everyone to participate."

The next Friday, we had "Two Different Socks Day" at Starwood Elementary. Lots of kids wore crazy, colorful socks with candy canes or cats. And if you'd forgotten, Mrs. Connor passed out unmatched socks at the afternoon assembly, so nobody was left out.

After talking through the microphone for a little bit about liking people just the way they are, Mrs. Connor put on some music and let us all dance in our socks.

"*¡Me encanta esto!*" Maria shouted, waving her arms.

We all loved it. Even Amy. I saw her twirling in the corner, wearing one striped sock and one polka-dotted sock. But she was dancing by herself. That didn't seem right.

SLIP! SLIDE! SLIP! SLIDE!

My special *zapatos* were back in the classroom. I had to slide to the rescue, not zoom. This time, I didn't bump into anyone.

"Hi, Freddie!" Amy's eyes twinkled. She was looking straight at me.

Jason followed me across the gym. So did Maria and Geraldo. Gio from Amy's class joined us. Soon, a whole group was swinging to the music together.

Don't Miss Freddie's Other Adventures!

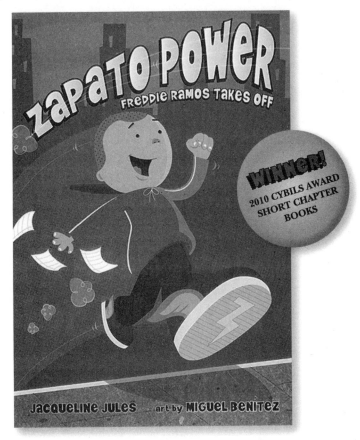

One day Freddie Ramos comes home from school and finds a strange box just for him. What's inside?

HC 978-0-8075-9480-3 • PB 978-0-8075-9479-7

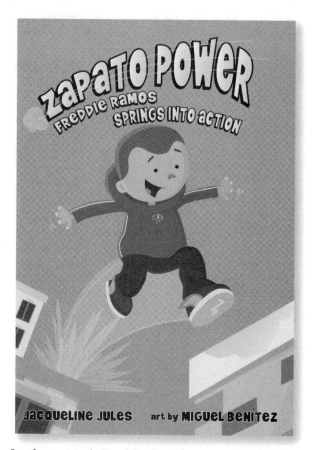

In this sequel, Freddie has shoes that give him
super speed. It's hard to be a superhero and a
regular kid at the same time, especially when
your shoes give you even more power!

PB 978-0-8075-9483-4

ZAPATO POWER

FREDDIE RAMOS ZOOMS TO THE RESCUE

JACQUELINE JULES   art by MIGUEL BENITEZ

Freddie's super-speedy adventures continue—
now he has superhero duties at school!

PB 978-0-8075-9484-1

When Freddie's zapatos go missing, how can
he use his Zapato Power?

HC 978-0-8075-9485-8 • PB 978-0-8075-9486-5

ZAPATO POWER
FREDDIE RAMOS
STOMPS THE SNOW

Jacqueline Jules   art by MIGUEL BENITEZ

There's a blizzard in Starwood Park—but the
weather can't stop a thief! It's up to Freddie
and his Zapato Power to save the day!

HC 978-0-8075-9487-2 • PB 978-0-8075-9496-4

ZAPATO POWER

FREDDIE RAMOS RULES NEW YORK

JACQUELINE JULES   art by MIGUEL BENITEZ

What happens when Freddie
outgrows his zapatos?

HC 978-0-8075-9497-1 • PB 978-0-8075-9499-5

How will Freddie learn to use his new super
hearing without becoming a super snoop?

HC 978-0-8075-9500-8 • PB 978-0-8075-9542-8

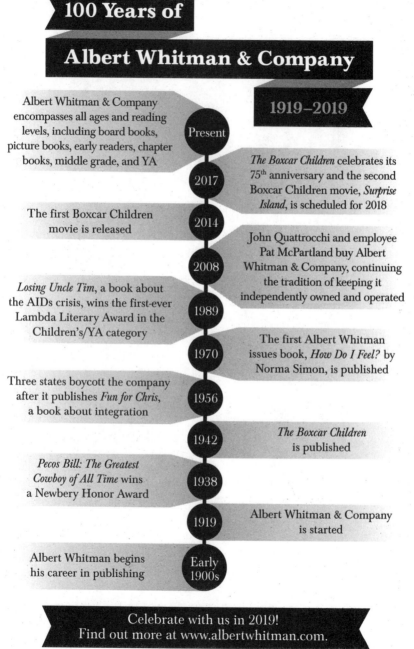

100 Years of

Albert Whitman & Company

1919–2019

Albert Whitman & Company encompasses all ages and reading levels, including board books, picture books, early readers, chapter books, middle grade, and YA

Present

2017 — *The Boxcar Children* celebrates its 75th anniversary and the second Boxcar Children movie, *Surprise Island*, is scheduled for 2018

The first Boxcar Children movie is released — **2014**

2008 — John Quattrocchi and employee Pat McPartland buy Albert Whitman & Company, continuing the tradition of keeping it independently owned and operated

Losing Uncle Tim, a book about the AIDs crisis, wins the first-ever Lambda Literary Award in the Children's/YA category — **1989**

1970 — The first Albert Whitman issues book, *How Do I Feel?* by Norma Simon, is published

Three states boycott the company after it publishes *Fun for Chris*, a book about integration — **1956**

1942 — *The Boxcar Children* is published

Pecos Bill: The Greatest Cowboy of All Time wins a Newbery Honor Award — **1938**

1919 — Albert Whitman & Company is started

Albert Whitman begins his career in publishing — **Early 1900s**

Celebrate with us in 2019!
Find out more at www.albertwhitman.com.